Cowgirl Kate and Cocoa

Rain or Shine

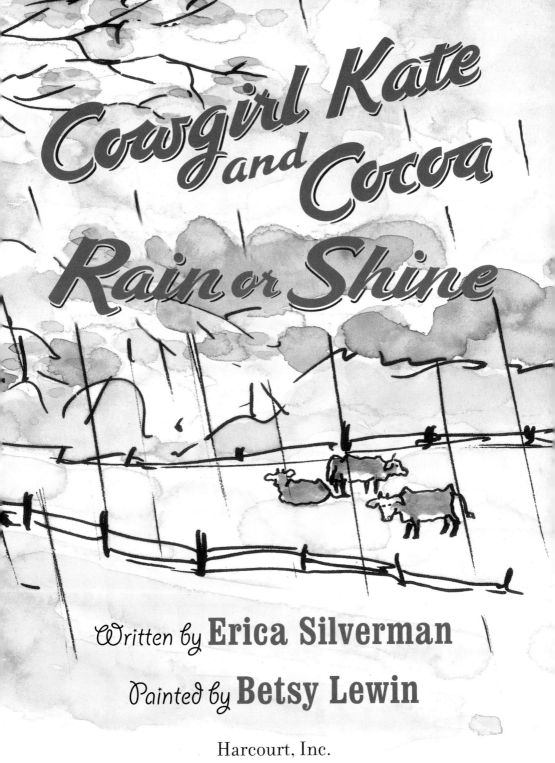

Cowgirl Kate and Cocoa

Rain or Shine

Written by **Erica Silverman**

Painted by **Betsy Lewin**

Harcourt, Inc.

Orlando   Austin   New York   San Diego   London

To Tricia Gardella, Hali Mundy, Lynne Olson,
Sylvia Patton, Karyl Thorn, and Judy Weedman,
my trusted advisors on all things horse —E. S.

To Chopper, who doesn't like the rain —B. L.

Text copyright © 2008 by Erica Silverman
Illustrations copyright © 2008 by Betsy Lewin

Requests for permission to make copies of any part of the work should be submitted online
at www.harcourt.com/contact or mailed to the following address: Permissions Department,
Harcourt, Inc., 6277 Sea Harbor Drive, Orlando, Florida 32887-6777.

www.HarcourtBooks.com

Library of Congress Cataloging-in-Publication Data
Silverman, Erica.
Cowgirl Kate and Cocoa: rain or shine/Erica Silverman; [illustrated by] Betsy Lewin.
p. cm.
Summary: Cowgirl Kate and her cowhorse, Cocoa, discover what it means to work, play,
and be together—rain or shine.
[1. Cowgirls—Fiction. 2. Horses—Fiction. 3. Rain and rainfall—Fiction.]
I. Lewin, Betsy, ill. II. Title. III. Title: Rain or shine.
PZ7.S58625Cok 2008
[E]—dc22   2006032363
ISBN 978-0-15-205384-0

First edition
H G F E D C B A

Printed in Singapore

The illustrations in this book were done in watercolors
on Strathmore one-ply Bristol paper.
The display type was hand-lettered by Georgia Deaver.
The text type was set in Filosofia Regular.
Color separations by SC Graphic Technology Pte. Ltd., Singapore
Printed and bound by Tien Wah Press, Singapore
Production supervision by Christine Witnik
Designed by April Ward

Chapter 1
Racing the Wind

Whoosh! went the wind.

"Let's race the wind!" said Cocoa.

"Not now," said Cowgirl Kate.

"We have to go to the hay shed
and count bales of hay."

Cowgirl Kate rode Cocoa to the hay shed.

She counted, "One, two, three..."

Cocoa nibbled.

"I counted fifty bales," said Cowgirl Kate.

"I counted fifty nibbles," said Cocoa.

Whooooooosh! went the wind.

"*Now* let's race the wind," said Cocoa.

"Not now," said Cowgirl Kate.

"We have to go to the south pasture and check the salt licks."

Cowgirl Kate rode Cocoa to the south pasture.

She checked the salt licks.

Cocoa licked the salt licks.

"The salt licks are getting low," said Cowgirl Kate.

"I will tell Dad."

Whoooooooooooooooooooooosh! went the wind.

"*Now* let's race the wind!" said Cocoa.

"Not now," said Cowgirl Kate.

"We have to go to the east pasture
  and check the fence."

Cowgirl Kate rode Cocoa to the east pasture.

She checked the fence.

Cocoa nudged it.

"I don't see any breaks," said Cowgirl Kate.

"Neither do I," said Cocoa.

Whoooooooooooooooooooooooooooooosh!
went the wind.
Suddenly the sky grew dark.
CLAP! CRASH! BOOM!
Cocoa's eyes opened wide.
His ears went back.
"Nnnnnneighhhhh!" he squealed.

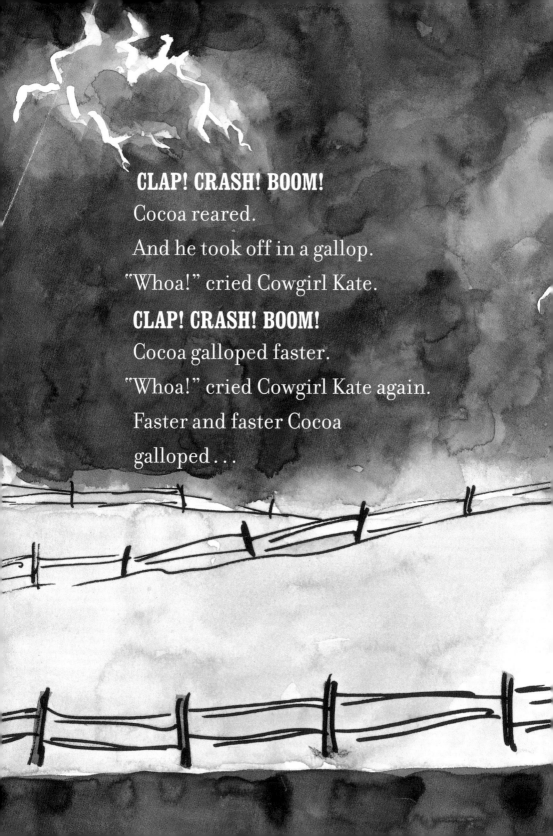

CLAP! CRASH! BOOM!
Cocoa reared.
And he took off in a gallop.
"Whoa!" cried Cowgirl Kate.
CLAP! CRASH! BOOM!
Cocoa galloped faster.
"Whoa!" cried Cowgirl Kate again.
Faster and faster Cocoa
galloped...

. . . all the way back to the barn.

Cowgirl Kate slid out of the saddle.

"Cocoa," she said,

"that noise was just thunder.

There was nothing to be afraid of."

Cocoa snorted.

"Afraid?" he said.

"I was not afraid!"

"But you ran *very, very* fast!" said Cowgirl Kate.

Cocoa raised his head high.
"Of course I ran fast," he said.
"I was racing the wind!"

Chapter 2
Cocoa's Cold

"Cocoa," said Cowgirl Kate,

"it's time for work."

Cocoa stuck his head out the barn window.

"But it's raining," he said.

"Rain or shine, the cows need us,"

said Cowgirl Kate.

"Every day?" asked Cocoa.

"Every day," said Cowgirl Kate. "What

would happen if a cow got sick?"

What would happen if a horse got sick?
thought Cocoa.
I think I will find out.

And he started to cough.
"Cah-cah-cah-cah."

Cowgirl Kate frowned.

"I hope you aren't getting sick," she said.

She looked in his eyes.

"Your eyes are not watery."

She checked his nose.
"Your nose is not drippy."

She listened to his chest.
"Your chest is not stuffy."
"*Cah-cah-cah-cah,*"
Cocoa coughed again.

Then he lay down.

Cowgirl Kate sighed.

"It is really too bad," she said.

"What is?" asked Cocoa.

"Today I have to ride through the timothy
grass," she said.

Cocoa's nose twitched.

"And I have to gather the apples
that the wind blew down," she said.

Cocoa smacked his lips.

"And then," said Cowgirl Kate,

"I have to go to the
cornfield."

"The cornfield?" squealed Cocoa.
"How will you get there without me?"
"I guess I will ride Dad's horse, Jumper,"
   said Cowgirl Kate.
   And she left the barn.
   Cocoa thought about Cowgirl Kate
   riding Jumper. He thought about
   timothy grass, and apples,
   and corn.

"Wait!" he called.

He scrambled up onto his hooves.

He hurried after Cowgirl Kate.

"I am all better!" he said.

"I am ready to work!"

"Are you sure?" asked Cowgirl Kate.

"It's still raining."

Cocoa raised his head high.

"Rain or shine," he said, "the cows need us."

Chapter 3
Prancing in the Rain

"I'm tired of staying inside," said Cocoa.

"I want to go out and play."

"It's still raining," said Cowgirl Kate.

"Let me put on your rain sheet."

"No!" cried Cocoa.

"I look silly in my rain sheet!"

"Jumper is wearing *his* rain sheet,"
said Cowgirl Kate.

"He looks silly," said Cocoa.

"But he'll stay dry," said Cowgirl Kate.

"I'd rather get wet!" said Cocoa.
And he trotted outside.

Rain fell on Cocoa. He shook it off.

He kicked up his hooves.

He pranced into the corral.

He pranced past Jumper.

He pranced—

SPLAT! SPLASH!—

into a puddle.

Rain fell harder.

It soaked Cocoa's coat.

It drenched his mane.

Cold raindrops rolled down his neck.

Cocoa shivered.

He looked at Jumper.

Jumper was not dripping wet.

He was not shivering.

Jumper does not look silly at all,

thought Cocoa, *he looks dry*.

Cocoa trotted back into the barn.

"You look like a wet mop," said Cowgirl Kate.

"I feel like a wet mop," said Cocoa.

Cowgirl Kate rubbed him down.

She wrung the water out of his tail.

She brushed the mud out of his mane.

"That's better," she said.

"Yes," said Cocoa.

"And *now* I will wear my rain sheet."

Cowgirl Kate put on his rain sheet.

"Cocoa," she said,

"you look good in your rain sheet."

She held up a mirror.

Cocoa whinnied.

"Yes," he agreed.

"And I look *much* better than Jumper."

Chapter 4
Chasing the Rainbow

Cocoa peeked into Cowgirl Kate's window.

"Wake up!" he said.

"The rain has stopped."

Cowgirl Kate opened her eyes.

"Yeehaw!" she shouted.

Cowgirl Kate got dressed.
Then she crawled through the window
and climbed onto Cocoa's back.

"Giddyup!" she called.

Cocoa trotted to the south pasture.

"Moo, moo," mooed the cows.

"Moo, moo, moo."

"The cows sure are moo-ing," said Cocoa.

"The cows always moo," said Cowgirl Kate.

"Yes," said Cocoa,

"but they moo even more after the rain."

Cowgirl Kate sniffed the air.

"The air sure smells fresh," she said.

"You always say the air smells fresh,"
   said Cocoa,

"Yes," said Cowgirl Kate,

"but it smells even fresher after the rain."

Cocoa nibbled some grass.

"The grass sure tastes sweet," he said.

"You always say the grass tastes sweet,"
 said Cowgirl Kate.

"Yes," said Cocoa,

"but it tastes even sweeter after the rain."

"Look, Cocoa," cried Cowgirl Kate,

"there's a rainbow!"

"Let's go!" squealed Cocoa.
"Let's find the pot of oats at the end of
   the rainbow!"
   And off he went at a brisk trot.

"Cocoa," said Cowgirl Kate,

"we will never reach the end of that rainbow."

"Yes, we will!" cried Cocoa.

On and on he trotted.

On and on and *on* he trotted.

Finally, he stopped.

"The rainbow keeps moving away," he said.

"Rainbows are like that," said Cowgirl Kate.

Cocoa's head drooped.

"Then I will never find the pot of oats
    at the end of the rainbow," he said.

"Maybe not," said Cowgirl Kate.

"But I know where we can find another one."

She rode Cocoa back to the barn.

She prepared warm oats.

She added molasses.

Cocoa snorted.

"That is not a *pot* of oats," he said.

"That is a *bucket* of oats."

But he gobbled them all up.

"Yum!" he said.

"Warm oats and molasses taste
even better after the rain."
Cowgirl Kate smiled.
"I guess everything is better
after the rain," she said.
"Not everything," said Cocoa.
He nudged her gently.
"You and I," he said,
"rain or shine . . ."

"*we* are always just right."